Quilliam
Needs a Hug

Story and Illustrations by Dr. Kelleyerin Clabaugh

AuthorHouse™
1663 Liberty Drive
Bloomington, IN 47403
www.authorhouse.com
Phone: 833-262-8899

Because of the dynamic nature of the Internet, any web addresses or
links contained in this book may have changed since publication and
may no longer be valid. The views expressed in this work are solely those
of the author and do not necessarily reflect the views of the publisher,
and the publisher hereby disclaims any responsibility for them.

This book is printed on acid-free paper.

ISBN: 978-1-6655-6621-6 (sc)
ISBN: 978-1-6655-6622-3 (hc)
ISBN: 978-1-6655-6623-0 (e)

Library of Congress Control Number: 2022913789

Print information available on the last page.

Published by AuthorHouse 08/19/2022

authorHOUSE®

For Chloe and Cooper

When Quilliam was a baby
he knew his family loved him very much.

Deep in their den
his mom would wrap her arms around him
and squeeze him tight.

Back then his quills were soft like hair.

3

But Quilliam had been on his
own for a while.
He missed his family and their embrace.

As he got older, his quills hardened
into long sharp spines all over his back.

He did not seem to have control over them.

When he was scared they stood straight up.

6

When he was excited they stood straight up.

When he sneezed they stood straight up.

And when he was sad
and really needed a hug
they stood straight up
and poked anyone who came near him.

Quilliam was frustrated and lonely.

He could not seem to control his emotions
and he certainly could not control his quills.

Quilliam's friends could tell that he was upset.

At first they tried to hug him.
But he always seemed to hurt them
even though he did not mean to.

His friends were worried about him.
But they did not know how to get closer to him.

One day Quilliam was walking along the river
when he tripped over a log.

The bank was steep and
Quilliam tumbled over and over
until he landed with a muddy splash
upside down on the edge of the river.

Quilliam squirmed but he could not turn over.
His quills were stuck deep in the mud.

His soft pink belly was exposed.
He remembered his father's warning
"Never let anyone see your soft side."

He felt vulnerable and scared.
There were crocodiles in the water
and he was not in a position to defend himself.

Quilliam's friends heard him crying
and ran to the river to help.

Harriette the Hippo rushed from the deep water chasing the crocodiles away with her big tusks.

Once they realized their friend was okay
they all started laughing.

Quilliam looked pretty ridiculous
upside down in the mud
with his bald tummy exposed.

They had never seen him like this.

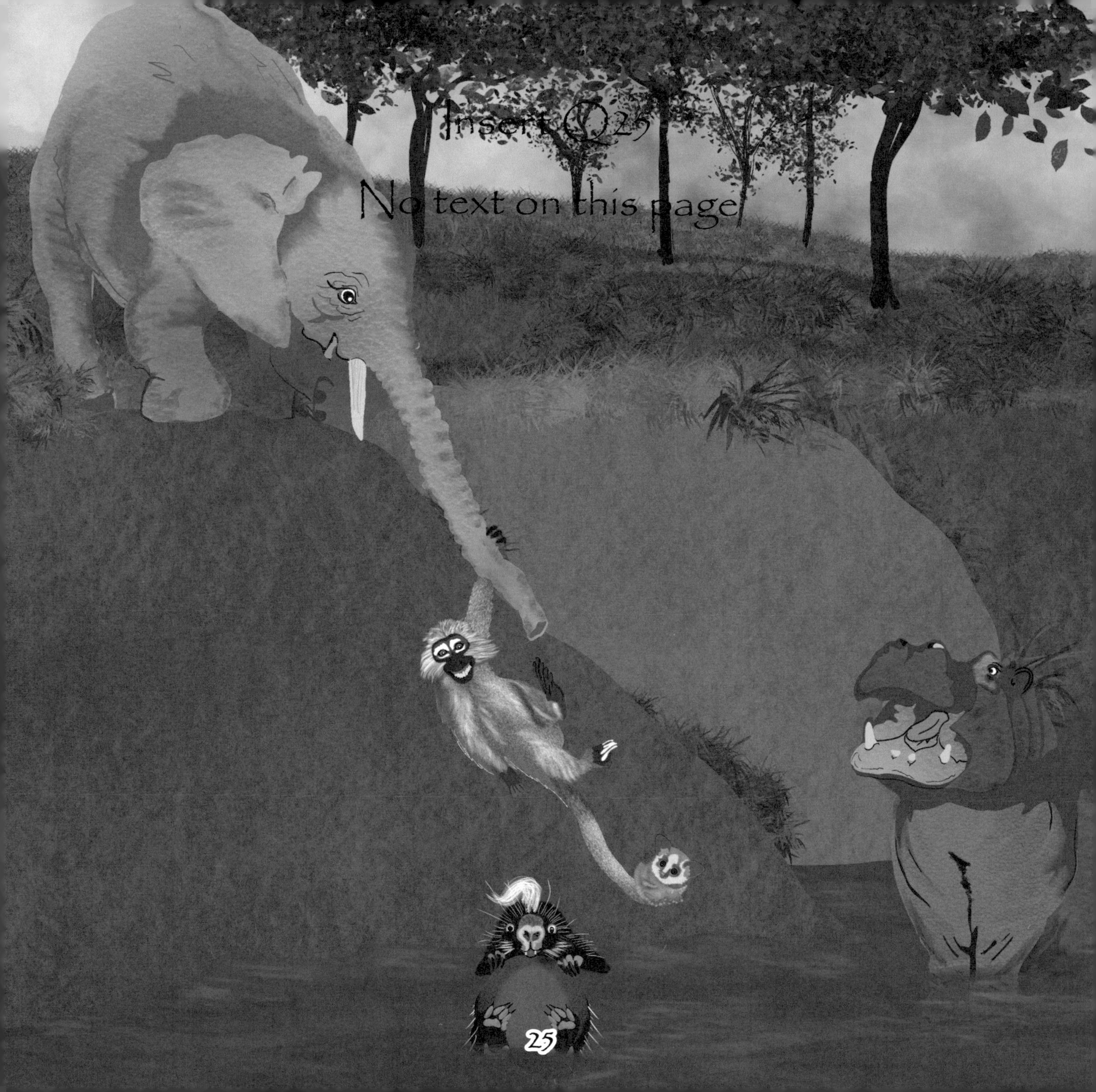
Insert Q25
No text on this page

Quilliam's friend the bush baby
crawled onto his belly
and wrapped his arms around him.

Quilliam sighed.
This was his first hug in years
and he REALLY needed it.

And then Quilliam realized,
you are vulnerable
when you let someone see your soft side.

But it is also how you let your friends
get close enough to love you.

DID YOU KNOW?

The Bush baby is nocturnal.
It sleeps during the day
and is active at night.
It sounds like a human baby crying.

The Vervet Monkey is arboreal
meaning it lives in the trees.
Vervets live in a group called a troup.

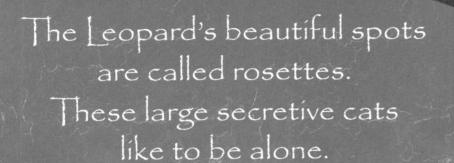

The Leopard's beautiful spots
are called rosettes.
These large secretive cats
like to be alone.

The African Crested Porcupine
cannot shoot its quills.
Instead it runs backwards
to poke predators with its spines.

Hippos are very territorial.
Males open their mouths wide
to show off their big teeth
when other animals get too close.

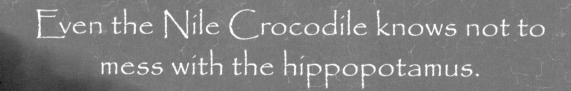

Even the Nile Crocodile knows not to
mess with the hippopotamus.

Printed in the United States
by Baker & Taylor Publisher Services